The Bradford Family
ADVENTURES
Daniel's Big Surprise

by

Jerry B. Jenkins

MOODY PRESS

CHICAGO

ISBN: 0-8024-0805-2

1 2 3 4 5 6 Printing/LC/Year 94 93 92 91 90

Printed in the United States of America

To my brother Jeff

Contents

1

One-on-One

Daniel Bradford jumped from the top step of the school bus, his blond hair flying. He hit the gravel at the side of the road on the dead run. The driver had scolded him many times for doing it. He had even got in trouble with his parents for it. But this was the last day of fifth grade. What could Mr. Gaylor do? Keep Daniel off the bus until the fall?

He chuckled as he sprinted up the road. Pulling a rubber-coated baseball from his backpack, he pretended he was taking long throws from his favorite ballplayer, Buck Spangler. Ooh, it felt good to be out of school!

He passed the mailbox with *Robert Bradford* painted on the side. Then he heard his mother's station wagon come around the far curve.

He raced to see if he could reach the garage door before she pushed the control button to raise it. But she beat him. He skidded to a stop and dropped his head in mock frustration. She smiled at him as she drove in.

Daniel pulled away from her hug, even though he liked the feel of her cool white hospital volunteer's uniform against his cheek.

"Aw, Daniel," she said. "Don't ever get so big you won't let your mom hug you."

She looked sad, but her blue eyes twinkled. He'd never admit it, because he would rather have looked like his father—with dark eyes and black hair—but he didn't really mind taking after his mother.

She must have known Daniel wanted to talk to her about something important. He slumped into a chair at the table and held his face in his hands. She pulled her chair close to his and sat down.

"What are you thinking about, Dan?" she asked. He liked it when she called him Dan. It made him feel older—like when she called his dad Bob.

But his dad was part of the problem. So were Jim and Maryann, his big brother and sister. And even his mother.

He looked up at her, but he didn't know how to say it. Sometimes, even though she was his mother, he felt kind of shy when she waited for him to say something.

"Well, I guess you're busy," he said, starting to get up.

"Just a minute, young man," she said. "I can tell you want to talk. And we have a few minutes before your brother and sister get home. Dad's taking us all out tonight to celebrate the end of school and the end of my job until fall. I don't have to worry about anything but changing my clothes. So tell me what's on your mind."

Daniel looked down at his running shoes. "How come you didn't have any more kids?" he blurted out.

His mother laughed. He didn't like that. He knew she didn't mean anything by it. But he always hated it when his father or his mother or his sister laughed at him. He didn't smile.

"Daniel," she said, "I'm afraid we've waited too long. Anyway, we're happy with our family just the way it is. Aren't you?"

Daniel knew his mother would know his answer if he said nothing. So he said nothing. She put her hand on his shoulder.

"Dan," she said soothingly, "your big brother and sister love you so much."

"I know," he said, "but they're in high school."

"They spend a lot of time with you—more than most big brothers and sisters would."

"But they don't understand me."

Daniel knew his mother wouldn't be able to answer that one. He didn't think she understood him either. She helped him off with his backpack and went to change clothes. He wandered out through the garage to the driveway and began to shoot baskets.

He knew he should feel lucky. His father was a test pilot in the Air Force. He had a dangerous job. He spent a lot of time working with the space program. His work took him to Florida at least once a month. But when he was home he was a good father.

Their six acres and huge house had been bought when Daniel was in kindergarten. He loved being able to run around the big spread. But Daniel knew that when they moved out here was when he had started to feel lonely.

His brother and sister, nice as they were, were just too much older to really be his friends.

His school friends had drifted away. They weren't able to come from town to visit him. Also his family had moved to a new church. There were a few kids he liked, but none with whom he had really built friendships.

Daniel missed his sixth basket in a row. He angrily bounced the ball high off the concrete drive. He caught it and sat down gloomily on the ground. He knew what the problem was. He wanted a brother.

He had a brother, of course. But he wanted one his own age—maybe a little younger.

The horn of his brother's Camaro startled Daniel. He jumped up and out of the way as Jim swung into the driveway. "Hey, little man!" Jim shouted as he slammed the door. He was tall and dark like his father.

"Hi, Danny!" Maryann called, getting out of the other

side and heading toward the house. "You may, as of this moment, begin calling me a sophomore," she said.

Daniel tried to smile at her. She was being nice and friendly as usual. But he wasn't in the mood for it.

"Shoot a few hoops?" Jim asked. He set his books on top of his car and swiped the basketball from Daniel's hands.

"Nah," Daniel said, slowly getting up.

"C'mon, Dan!" He had been a starting forward on the high school team for two years now. "Your ball!" he called. With that he fired a chest pass that nearly knocked Daniel over.

Daniel really didn't want to play. But when Jim came charging toward him he whipped the ball back at him. Jim wasn't ready for it, and it bounded off him and back to Daniel.

"Oh, ho!" Jim shouted, awkwardly flying past Daniel. "Think you're pretty crafty, huh?"

Daniel couldn't hide a smile. He moved under the basket and made an easy layup. Now he knew he'd have to play one-on-one with Jim whether he really wanted to or not.

"Where'd you learn *that* little trick, Big Dan?" Jim asked. He gathered in the ball and moved out deep again for another long jump shot.

Daniel didn't answer, not wanting to admit that he hadn't done it on purpose. He turned toward the basket just as Jim's shot rolled around in the rim and out. He beat Jim to the rebound and dribbled past him.

He knew Jim could have stolen the ball from him as he went by. But Jim always played at about half speed with Daniel. In fact, that's why Daniel felt so good about his first basket. He actually had beaten a soon-to-be high school senior on a trick play. Maybe he hadn't planned it, but it had worked anyway.

They were tied at a basket each. They always played to five. Daniel usually felt good if he scored twice.

Jim scrambled back to defend against Daniel's drive to the basket. So Daniel tried to surprise him again. He just threw up a shot without stopping, jumping, or anything. Swish!

Jim stood smiling at his younger brother, his hands on his hips. "I don't believe this!" he said. "How'd you become a hot shot all of a sudden?"

But Daniel was following his own shot. He couldn't remember ever having led his brother in any game, even though Jim was careful never to shut him out the way he could have.

Suddenly Daniel wanted to win this game, to beat Jim for the first time. "It's your shot, big guy," he said quickly. "You talking or playing?"

He tossed the ball to Jim, who stood staring at him, wide-eyed. Daniel slapped at the ball before Jim had a chance to dribble. The ball hit Jim's foot and bounced right into Daniel's hands. That meant he didn't have to take the ball deep like he would have if Jim had shot.

Daniel spun toward the basket and tossed in a bank shot from about six feet. Jim jumped over him from behind to try to block it. He came down heavily on Daniel, knocking him to the ground.

"You little turkey!" Jim said laughing. "You're creaming me. You all right?" Daniel nodded. "Then give me that ball."

"You fouled me, right?" Daniel said. "So it's my ball again, right?"

Jim shook his head slowly. "My own rules are catching up with me," he said.

Daniel took the ball out and dribbled carefully up to Jim, who kept Daniel from getting too close to the basket. Jim seemed to be fully into the game now. But he was still giving Daniel room to play, as he always did.

As Daniel dribbled and looked for an opening to move around Jim, he asked, "What's the score? You counting that shot you made before I knew we were playing?"

Jim straightened up for an instant to think about it. While he hesitated, Daniel shot over him. The ball bounced in and out and around and in. All of a sudden, Daniel was one basket from winning.

2

Miracle Shot

"Now I am!" Jim shouted, enjoying himself. "Counting my first shot, that's what. Otherwise I'm down four to zero."

He faked a pass to Daniel. Then he faked to his right, making Daniel move that way. By the time Daniel recovered, Jim had slipped past him on the left and scored an easy lay-up.

Daniel took the ball back out deep. He wondered if Jim would give him room, as he normally did, to dribble and get off a shot. He didn't have long to wonder. As soon as he started toward the basket, Jim reached for the ball and batted it to the ground.

It bounced back up to Daniel, but as he continued the dribble, Jim slid over in front of him, making him stop. As he pulled up to shoot, Jim's hands were all over the ball. Daniel let it fly, but Jim stole it out of the air. He leaped to the hoop and slam dunked his third point.

Daniel was angry. He knew Jim could hold him scoreless for two more plays and beat him. So what? Couldn't Jim let up just a little? But Jim flipped Daniel the ball. Then he went into his fierce defense again.

The same thing happened. Jim was all over Daniel and the ball. He couldn't even get a shot off before Jim smothered him and scored.

Daniel was fighting the sobs that rose up in his throat. He hadn't asked for this dumb game! All he wanted was a chance to win. He knew that in the early part of the game he had simply taken his brother off guard. Why couldn't Jim just let up a little now and give him a chance.

For the third straight time, Daniel was unable to move with the ball. Jim stole it and dribbled around, teasing him. Jim didn't take his shot. He made Daniel hustle to try to keep him from scoring.

"I don't think your first basket should count!" Daniel hollered, trying not to cry.

"OK, fair enough," Jim said. He stopped dead and pushed up a light shot. It popped the net without even touching the rim. *"That* ties it."

Daniel took the ball back once more. Within seconds Jim had it again. Now he seemed to relax, having scored four straight times. He needed just one more to win. Daniel tried to stay with Jim as he smoothly moved around the driveway with the ball.

Daniel knew that at any instant Jim could easily push through another shot. Or he could drive to the basket and score over his much smaller brother. But Jim didn't.

Then Jim did something silly, something he usually saved for those games when he had the ball and a big lead. He stepped back and lifted the ball over his head. Then he slammed it to the ground in front of Daniel.

Daniel backed up as the ball sailed over his head toward the basket. He was angry. If Jim wanted to make him feel bad, why didn't he just make an easy shot instead of trying something crazy?

Daniel turned to watch as the ball bounced short of the rim. Jim tried to push past and get the rebound. But Daniel beat Jim to it. He dribbled the ball back out, as Jim laughed.

"Why didn't you shoot?" Jim asked. "The ball never touched the rim or the backboard! You didn't need to bring it out! You could have scored! You would have won!"

Daniel was angry at himself for making such a mistake. He was so mad at Jim for making fun of him and not giving him a chance, that his eyes filled with tears. He wanted to yell at his big brother. But he couldn't think of anything to say.

Jim held his stomach and threw back his head to laugh louder. Daniel exploded! "I hate you!" he screamed. He slammed the ball to the ground next to Jim's feet. Jim skipped out of the way so it wouldn't smack him in the head.

As Daniel ran toward the garage, the ball arched high and came down on the back of the rim. It bounced high again. It came down onto the front of the rim. It angled neatly off the backboard and dropped silently through the net.

Daniel stopped as he reached the open garage door and stared. He was unable to enjoy his victory because of his anger. Jim laughed even louder when he saw what had happened, realizing Daniel had beaten him.

Daniel continued through the garage, eager to get to his room. He had been trying to beat Jim in that stupid game for years. Now he had done it, and Jim was just laughing at him.

He stormed in the back door just as pretty Maryann was coming out. "I beat Jim in basketball," Daniel said miserably, still scowling.

"Sure you did," she said. "You going to play for the Lakers next year?"

"I did!" he shouted, turning to face her.

"Whatever," she said, as if their basketball game was the last thing she cared about. "Mom wants you. She got a call from Mr. Gaylor."

Daniel's heart sank. He turned slowly to find his mother. He could hear Maryann in the driveway asking Jim what was so funny. Right then Daniel hated them both—not to mention the bus driver who didn't have anything better to do than get innocent kids in trouble.

"Daniel," his mother said, "I have to tell you I'm upset. Did you jump off the bus again while it was still moving?"

"No," he said angrily. "Old Man Gaylor won't open the door until he's been stopped for ten minutes."

"I have told you not to refer to your elders that way, young man, and I mean it."

"Sorry!"

"You don't sound like it. Now what did you do getting off the bus today?"

"I just jumped down the steps, that's all," he said, the tears starting again. "Why is everybody against me?"

"Nobody's against you, Daniel. But you've been told not to do that. It's dangerous."

"It's not!"

"Don't argue with me."

"It's not, Mom! I've never been hurt. The bus is stopped, and I just skip two steps, that's all."

She stared at him in silence, as if she couldn't imagine how such a thing could be that dangerous. But it had obviously upset the driver enough that he felt he needed to tell her about it. "The point remains that you disobeyed, Daniel. That means no TV this weekend."

"No TV!" he shouted. "There's three ball games on this weekend!"

"That's too bad. You've got to learn to obey."

Daniel ran upstairs to his room. He planned to slam the door. But he had been warned about that, too, and he decided against it. Just before he shut his door, he heard Jim telling his mother, "I'm serious. The kid beat me. He caught me flatfooted early. And then he beat me on a trick shot. I don't think he planned it, but he did it. He's really getting pretty good, you know."

Daniel enjoyed hearing Jim say that. But he still wished his big brother hadn't laughed at him.

And he wished his sister believed he beat Jim.

And he wished Old Man Gaylor hadn't told on him, especially on the last day of school.

And he wished his mother hadn't taken away his TV privileges for the weekend.

But most of all he wished his dad would get home soon. He was the only person in the family that Daniel didn't have something against right now. He wanted to talk to his dad. He wanted to calm down before they went to dinner, and to get over his crying and his anger so he could enjoy going out.

3

It Isn't Fair

Daniel awoke to a gentle knock on his door. He sat up quickly and noticed it was dark outside. He must have slept for hours. He was hungry.

"Come in," he said.

His dad entered with a smile and sat next to him on the bed. He clapped Daniel on the shoulder. "How's my big guy?" he asked.

"I'm OK. I beat Jim in basketball."

"Yeah!" his dad said. "That's what I heard!"

"He let me."

"That's not the way I heard it," Mr. Bradford said. "You were a little lucky maybe, but he didn't let you. No, sir!"

"How come you're home so late, Dad?"

"Oh, I've been home a while. We just didn't want to wake you until everyone got so hungry they couldn't wait any longer. You want to sleep some more, or are you ready to get some food in you?"

"I guess I'm ready."

"Something been bothering you today, son?"

"Yeah."

"You want to talk about it?"

"Nah."

"You sure?"

"Yeah."

"You know you can always talk to me, don't you, Daniel?"

"Yeah."

"You know I love you?"

"I know."

"You also know I don't like to hear that you've disobeyed, and that you've talked back to your mother."

Daniel didn't answer. Maybe it wasn't true that he could always talk to his dad. His dad would never believe him against his mother. Of course, he *had* disobeyed. And he *had* spoken angrily to her. But he didn't consider it actually talking back to her.

"She didn't have to tell me I couldn't watch the ball games, though, Dad."

"I'm sorry about that, Daniel. But you're getting a little too big for spankings, and we have to help you remember to obey."

Daniel started feeling miserable again. No one understood. "Please, Dad. If I promise . . ."

"Don't beg, Daniel. Your mother set the punishment, and I'm not going to change it. You can listen to the games on the radio."

"That's no fun!"

Mr. Bradford's thick eyebrows narrowed. And he looked disappointed. That hurt Daniel more than any spanking could have. It even hurt worse than the thought of not watching the ball games. "I'm sorry, Dad," he said. "I didn't mean to talk back to you."

His dad wrapped his arms around Daniel's shoulders and held him tight. "Thanks, Daniel. You know I want you to say the same thing to your mother."

"But I didn't really talk back to her, Dad."

There went those eyebrows again. Sometimes life just wasn't fair. "I'll tell her," he muttered.

"And mean it?" his dad asked.

"I'll try."

At the restaurant the conversation centered on Dad's work, Mom's summer, Jim's job at the local pool, and Maryann's boyfriend. Daniel's name came up a time or two, mostly in fun. Once Jim said, "I may not even make the team next year if the coach finds out I lost to Danny today."

Everyone laughed. Daniel tried to smile, but he didn't think it was so funny.

Maybe Jim was reacting the only way he knew how. Maybe he was trying to make Daniel feel good about himself. It wasn't working. He still felt lonely. He still wanted someone his own age to talk to and play with.

They were eating dessert by the time Mr. Bradford noticed that Daniel had been quiet during the whole meal. "Tell me about your week, Dan," he said. Daniel hated that. What did he mean "about his week"?

Daniel shrugged.

"C'mon, Dan," his dad said. "*Something* interesting must have happened in your life this week."

"School ended," he said, not intending to be funny. Everyone laughed.

"Anything else?" his dad asked. "Don't they always have special outings and things the last week of school?"

"We don't," Maryann interrupted. "Just tests and junk like that!"

Daniel shook his head. His mother looked away, as if giving up trying to get him to talk. His father, however, did not give up.

"Any outings? You go anywhere? Seems we signed a form a couple of weeks ago. What was that for?"

"That was for Monday," Daniel said. "It was boring."

"What was boring?" his dad asked. "Where'd you go?"

"To an orphanage."

"Oh, I remember that field trip," Maryann said. "They don't call it an orphanage anymore, Daniel. It's a children's home. And it wasn't boring, unless you had your eyes closed."

He glared at her. Why was she down on him all of a sudden?

"It was sad," she said. "Didn't you find it sad? Those poor kids!"

Everyone was looking at Daniel now. He was toying with his strawberry shortcake. The trip to the home *had* made him feel strange. Maybe Maryann was right. Maybe "bored" wasn't the word for it. It *had* made him feel uncomfortable, and he *had* wanted to get out of there. But he didn't know why.

He decided it was scary more than anything else. What a thought! To have to live in a big building with a bunch of kids and teacherlike people who weren't your parents. What if you never got any visitors, or if your best friend got adopted and never came to visit?

"Yeah, I guess it *was* kind of sad," Daniel admitted. "I didn't like it there. Many of the kids were different races. Some were Mexican, I think. How come there weren't that many white kids, except a couple of kids on crutches, Dad?"

"I'll answer that in a minute," Mr. Bradford said. "But let me get something straight first. You aren't saying that you disliked the place because there were black and Mexican children there, are you?"

"No, no! I was just telling you who was there. I didn't like it because it made me feel sort of scared."

"I know what you mean, Daniel," Maryann said. "It made me feel the same way. And very sad."

"Tell me why there aren't that many white kids, Dad," Daniel said.

His parents looked at each other, and Mrs. Bradford smiled. His dad put down his fork and folded his hands. "Mostly, I think it's because more white people are having smaller families. And they can afford to keep their babies.

What happens then is that there are a lot fewer babies born who can be adopted."

"A lot fewer white ones you mean?"

"Well, yes. And because most white people, when they want to adopt a child, want to adopt a white one."

"And a healthy one," Jim said.

"Fewer black and Latino families can afford to adopt," Mr. Bradford said. "So the children's homes have more of these children."

Daniel nodded. "It isn't fair, is it? I mean, isn't it selfish of white people to only want white kids and kids who aren't handicapped?"

Neither of his parents spoke for several seconds. Finally, his mother said, "That's not really for us to say. If a mom and dad want another child just like their own—and if they don't want the problems that could come from adding a child of another race, or one who needs more care than usual—that's up to them."

"But then what happens to all the rest?" Daniel asked. "Don't they need parents, too?"

"I'll tell you what else they need, Daniel," Jim said. "They need friends."

"They've got friends," Daniel said. "They've got each other."

"But that's all they've got," Maryann said. "They have their own school, their own playground—their own everything! They *do* need friends from outside the children's home."

"Yeah," Jim said. "Friends like you, Dan."

4

No Friends

A Bradford family tradition was for everyone to help with the yard work on Saturday mornings. Usually Daniel enjoyed it. But this Saturday Daniel was troubled.

His father was sawing branches from one of the bigger trees in the back lot. Jim was mowing the front yard. Maryann was helping their mother trim the hedge. Daniel was bagging clippings and carting them to the edge of the road.

He was glad the mower was loud so he wouldn't be expected to talk with Jim. He liked his brother all right. He was over his anger at Jim for laughing at him the night before. But still he was glum.

Jim turned off the mower and called Daniel over. His big brother was right in the middle of a row in the center of the yard. It didn't seem a good place to take a break. But Jim signaled that Daniel should follow him. When they got to the front step, Jim pointed where he wanted Daniel to sit.

Still puzzled, Daniel was glad for the rest. He sat wearily and wiped the sweat from his face. "Wait here a minute, pal," Jim said. "I'll be right back."

Jim didn't return after a few minutes. Daniel stood and

looked through the picture window in the living room, into the kitchen, and out the back window. Jim was in the backyard with a tray, a pitcher of lemonade, and glasses with ice. He was pouring for the rest of the family.

When he came around to the front again, Jim had just his own glass and Daniel's.

"Thanks," Daniel said.

Jim didn't say anything. He just sat next to Daniel and took a long drink. Then he pulled the visor cap from his head. He ran the back of his hand over his forehead. "Hot one today, eh, Dan?"

Daniel nodded.

"You haven't cracked a smile all morning," Jim said. "What's wrong?"

"Nothing. Just don't feel that happy, that's all."

"Got anything to be sad about?"

"Not really."

"You really don't, you know," Jim said. "Think about it. You've got everything a kid could want or need."

That only made Daniel feel guilty. Was he ungrateful to wish he had a brother his own age? How could he tell Jim that? He just scowled and drank his lemonade.

"Hey, Dan," Jim said, "I'm sorry about laughing at you last night. But you know, I wasn't really laughing at you. Well, maybe I was. It's just that when you didn't take the easy shot to beat me after I missed my bounce shot, I figured I couldn't get luckier than that. I really should have lost right then. And even though your winning shot was lucky, you deserved to win."

"No, I didn't."

"Of course you did," Jim said.

"No. Anybody who forgets to shoot when he has the chance really doesn't deserve to win."

"You know why I was so relieved when you didn't score at first? Because you've been getting closer and closer to beating me."

"You could score every time you have the ball if you

wanted to. And you could keep me from scoring every time I have the ball. You proved that when you had to. That's what made me so mad. Why play hard only when I'm about to win?"

"Can't pull anything over on you, can I?" Jim said. "You're right. I usually give you enough room to score a little. But lately I've had to play a lot harder to keep you from winning. Last night I had to play as if I were in a game."

"I know. I couldn't do a thing, and it made me mad."

"I guess I shouldn't have done that, Dan. It wasn't fair. But at least you know that I had to play my best to keep you from scoring. I've been worried about you beating me someday. And when I missed that bounce shot, you deserved to win."

"I *did* win!"

"How well I know. So what're you so upset about?"

"Nothing."

"C'mon, Daniel. I know you better than that. I know when something's on your mind."

Daniel finished his lemonade. He twirled the melting cubes in the bottom of his glass. He didn't really want to tell Jim. But it was nice that he admitted he shouldn't have played so hard the night before. He could hardly believe that Jim had been worried for a long time about losing to him.

"Do you realize," Daniel said finally, "that I don't have any friends?"

Jim finished his drink and set the glass down on the step beside him. He ran both hands back through his hair and replaced his cap. Daniel worried that that meant Jim was ready to go back to mowing. Now that he had got it out, he wanted to talk about it.

Jim leaned forward and rested his elbows on his knees. "No friends?" he repeated.

Daniel nodded.

"None?"

"None."

"How about those guys at church?"

24

"That's only on Sunday. None of them even go to my school."

"But didn't you have your whole class out here once?"

"Yeah, once. That's no good. You don't get to know anyone. No one can come back because their parents have to bring them. Or Dad has to take them back, or something. It's just not worth all the trouble."

Jim squinted at Daniel. Daniel felt good because he seemed to really be listening. "Are you worried that maybe you're not worth the trouble for someone to make the effort to be your friend?"

Daniel didn't think so. He hadn't really thought of that. He shook his head.

"That's good," Jim said, "because that would be crazy. You'd be someone's good friend."

"If I had the chance," Daniel said.

"Who are you blaming?" Jim said.

"What do you mean?"

"Just what I said. If it's not your fault, whose fault is it? It has to be someone's fault."

"I don't know."

"Sure you do. Dad?"

"Do I think it's Dad's fault I don't have any friends? I don't know. I don't think so. Why would it be his fault?"

"Because he moved us out here. Away from our neighborhood. Away from our friends. You had plenty of friends before, didn't you?"

"Yeah. That's because all the kids on our block went to the same school—and most of us to the same church, too."

"You know what, Daniel? I didn't like moving out here, either."

"You didn't?"

"I sure didn't."

"Did *you* blame Dad?"

"Sort of. I blamed God even more."

"You blamed God?" Daniel said.

Jim nodded. "Because I prayed that it wouldn't happen.

I knew Mom and Dad were thinking and talking about it. But I wanted so badly to stay in our neighborhood that I just knew God wouldn't let them move."

"But He did."

"That's right. You know why? Because He knew it would be better for the family. We'd be closer. We'd care about each other more, have more time for each other. We'd learn more important things—things like trust and responsibility. You know, I don't think I ever would have made the basketball team if we were still living in town."

"But God didn't answer your prayer then?"

"Sure He answered it. He said no. Because He knows best. Mom and Dad went on and on about how much we'd love having more room and a slower life. I dreaded telling them that I didn't want to go."

"Did you ever tell them?" Daniel asked.

"No, and I'm glad I didn't. Because by the time we were here for a few months, I couldn't have been happier."

"I never knew that," Daniel said."

"Neither did Mom or Dad. And I'd appreciate it if you didn't tell them."

"I won't."

Daniel couldn't see how his talk with Jim had helped any. He still didn't have a friend or a brother his own age. Yet he couldn't get his mind off the children's home.

"Have you prayed about your problem, Dan?" Jim asked.

"Yes."

"Really?"

"Some."

"Really?"

"A little."

"Really?"

"Not much."

"That's what I thought. What else is bothering you?"

"I can't get my mind off those kids at the home. I mean, I didn't think about much of anything when I was there except how scary it was. And how I wanted to go home. But after what everybody said at dinner last night, I haven't been able to quit thinking about it."

Jim trotted into the house with the empty glasses. When he came out, he smacked Daniel on the back and said, "Let's get this finished. Then I want to tell you what you and I are going to do this afternoon."

"You mean you're not going to be watching the game?"

"I can skip one. I've got a better idea."

"What is it?"

"You'll see."

5

A Visit to the Home

"Where are we going?" Daniel asked Jim in the Camaro an hour later. Jim had told him to shower and dress nicely.

"Just listen to the radio, kid," Jim said, tuning in the game. But Daniel couldn't think about the game, not even when Buck Spangler was batting. He just kept trying to guess where his big brother was taking him.

Finally, they arrived downtown. Jim pulled into the high-fenced parking lot of the State Home for Children complex. He turned the car off and shifted in his seat to face Daniel.

"What would you think about this place to keep you busy over the summer?"

Daniel didn't know what he meant. "If you mean do I want to stay here, no, I don't."

Jim laughed. "Of course you wouldn't stay here. But it could be the answer to your problem."

"Which problem?"

"There are plenty of kids here. Seems at least one could be your friend. Then there's the fact that both your sister and I have summer jobs. We won't be around much. It could get lonely out at the house with not much to do."

"I have plenty to do," Daniel said, a little worried about just what Jim had in mind.

"Suit yourself," Jim said. "It was just an idea." He started the car.

"Well, what were you thinking?" Daniel asked. "What did you think I was supposed to do here?"

"I just thought we'd go in and look. Just you and me. We could ask around. Find out what somebody your age could do here a few hours a day. It's not far from home, so you could ride your bike."

"Mom would never let me come into the city on my ten-speed."

"She might if you were careful and weren't gone long. You could always come home before dark. And I'll bet there's a place here where you could keep your bike."

"I still don't know what you're thinking, Jim."

"I'm not thinking anything. I just thought maybe you'd want to come back here and see if there was anything you could do with these kids. You want a friend. You need something to do. And you can't get this place and these kids off your mind. Am I right?"

"Yeah, but what if they don't let me, or if there's nothing I can do, or—"

"Then we just jump back in the car and head home. OK?"

Daniel thought about it a while. "OK," he said finally. Jim turned the car off again. Daniel's knees felt weak as he and his brother mounted the steps and entered a long, dark hall to look for the administration office. He wasn't sure what Jim was getting him into. But it felt good that Jim cared enough to even think about it.

He had a funny feeling in the pit of his stomach when they were asked to sit in huge vinyl-covered chairs and wait for the weekend administrator. People in the office glanced at them. Daniel imagined that they assumed he was a new boy being brought there to live.

Eventually they were called in to see Miss Simpson, a tall, bony woman with short, brown hair and black, horn-rimmed glasses. She seemed to force a smile as she asked how she could help Jim.

"This is my brother, Daniel," Jim said. "We were just wondering if there was anything he could do around here this summer to help out."

Miss Simpson stared without expression at Jim, as if she expected him to explain more. When he didn't, she said, "I don't understand. Is he looking for a place to stay?"

"Oh, no," Jim said. "Nothing like that. We live outside of town. He would come in everyday to help out, work with the kids, play with them, do chores, whatever."

Miss Simpson still had not looked at Daniel. That made him feel uneasy. "We have nearly three hundred elementary-age children in this facility, Mr., ah—"

"Bradford. Jim Bradford."

"Yes, Mr. Bradford. We have many children and a large staff. We really don't have need for anyone to help with the chores."

"Is there a volunteer staff of any kind?"

"Yes. For high schoolers and up." She finally turned and looked at Daniel. "I'm assuming this young man is not even in junior high yet."

"Going into sixth grade," Jim said.

Miss Simpson stood and began moving toward the door. "Then I'm afraid there's nothing he would be able to do here."

Daniel started to get up, too, feeling almost relieved. He liked the place even less after meeting Miss Simpson. For some reason, Jim stayed right where he was and didn't even follow Miss Simpson with his eyes.

"Are you saying that there aren't even visiting hours?" He directed his question to the empty chair behind Miss Simpson's desk.

"Visiting hours are from two to four everyday," she said.

"Any restrictions?" Jim asked, still with his back to her.

"I don't follow you, Mr. Bradford."

He swung around to face her. "I mean, do the visitors have to be related to the children?"

"These children, sir, are very rarely, *very* rarely, visited by anyone, let alone relatives."

"Then Daniel could visit them everyday?"

Daniel spoke up. "I'd visit the ones who play by themselves," he said. "The ones who don't seem to have any friends. Maybe someone could tell me who they are. And I could visit a different one each day. Just play with them for a couple of hours."

Miss Simpson still didn't seem pleased with the idea, but she shut her door and returned to her desk. Just what Jim had been trying to get her to do. Now she ignored Jim and turned her full attention to Daniel.

"Were you on one of those field trips recently?" she asked. He nodded. "And you went away feeling bad for the children. Is that it?"

"Well, not exactly. I felt bad, but I didn't know why. At first I just thought I wanted to get out of here. But after I talked about it with my brother and sister, and mom and dad, I knew I felt sorry for the kids."

"Let me tell you something. What was your name again?" Daniel told her. "Yes, Daniel. No one needs to feel sorry for these children. They are much better off than they have ever been. They come from bad homes. When they are adopted or taken into foster homes, they often wind up in places worse than they came from. We get more than a few back."

"You get them back?" Daniel asked.

"Sad to say, some of the more abusive homes are foster homes," she said. "Most of these children would rather be here than where they came from, or where they might go, whether they know it or not."

"Do you mean that they don't want a friend to visit them? Not even the loneliest ones?"

"Oh, they might," she said. "They just might. But one

31

thing you should be very clear about. Anything you do for or with any of these children should not be out of a feeling that you're doing something for them. Don't pity them. You'll be the better for your daily visits here. Probably more so than they will."

"Then I can come?" Daniel asked. He was not quite sure why he was so eager to do it now when he wasn't a few minutes before. Maybe because she'd made it a challange.

"You may," she said, "if it's all right with the regular administrator. I'll leave a message for him. You may call him on Monday morning."

"What will I be able to do with the kids?" Daniel asked.

"Between two and four on weekdays, you may do anything you wish, within reason. Anything here in the complex, that is."

"Who will I visit first?"

"That will be up to Mr. Epton. He'll tell you when you call on Monday. You must bring a parent with you that first day. And there will be many forms to fill out and rules to obey."

In the car, Daniel asked Jim if he thought his mother would appove.

"Are you kidding, little man?" he asked. "By two o'clock every day this summer, she'll be more than glad to get rid of you."

"Jim?"

"Yeah?"

"That was a good idea. Thanks for taking me."

"Don't mention it."

"I don't like Miss Simpson very much, though."

"Not real charming, was she?"

"Nope."

"Daniel, a woman like that wouldn't even be able to get a job in a children's home like the one our church sends money to. The people who work there are there because they love the kids and care about them. They are dedicated people."

32

"Doesn't anybody care about the kids at the state home?"

"I think they do. And I'm sure you'll run into lots of nice people on the staff. You're gonna look forward to this and have fun with it, aren't you?"

"I think so," Daniel said.

"Like having a brother your own age?"

"I hope so."

Daniel thought that Monday would never come soon enough.

6

The Apology

In spite of their closeness, the Bradford family always seemed to have short tempers on Sunday mornings.

Riding to and from church, even in the roomy station wagon, usually proved to be a problem for the two high schoolers and Daniel.

But for some reason, this Sunday was different. Daniel was ready for church early. His mother didn't have to ask him to change into something more dressy. Except for wearing no tie, he looked as dressed up as Jim and his dad.

While he sat on the hood of the car waiting for the rest of the family, Daniel finished up the remaining questions in his lesson book. He wasn't sure himself why he seemed so on top of things. His mother was astounded.

When the rest of the family was getting into the car, Daniel heard his mother tell his dad, ". . . and I didn't even have to remind him about bringing his Bible."

Mr. Bradford smiled but didn't say anything.

"What're you so happy about today?" Jim asked.

Daniel shrugged and smiled.

"Excited about tomorrow, I'll bet," Jim said.

Daniel shrugged again. It did seem that things had become better for him. There was no squabbling, no shouting, no pouting on the way to church. He listened in class. He even answered a few questions. He sang loudly during church and listened carefully during the prayer and the sermon.

For some reason, Daniel felt a great responsibility about his new job. He wanted to be ready. He wanted to be at his best. That was it. He was treating his opportunity as a summer job. What he really wanted, as much as having something worthwhile and important to do to fill his time, was the chance to find a friend. Maybe two. Maybe many.

Daniel ran from the church, shouting good-byes to his classmates. His father allowed him to take the car keys and start the car. He could turn the key, step on the gas pedal, start the engine, turn on the air conditioner, and tune the radio to the ball game. He was never allowed to touch the gearshift lever.

Daniel could hardly breathe in the ovenlike station wagon until the air conditioner kicked in. By the time the rest of the family got in the car, it was cool and the ball game was on.

During a commercial, Daniel told his father about his Sunday school lesson. He even told him about one of the girls in the class whose father was in the hospital. But then Daniel's mother said something that nearly ruined his day.

"I hope you don't think your good behavior is going to make me change my mind about you watching television this afternoon," she said.

Daniel was hurt. He felt insulted. He had never given it a thought. He knew he couldn't watch, and he was disappointed. But he had decided to just accept it and listen to the double header on the radio.

He fought the tears that welled up in his eyes. *How could Mom say such a thing?* he wondered. But she was staring straight ahead and couldn't see that his face had turned red. He dropped his head to stare at the floor.

Jim noticed, however. He quickly reached over and patted Daniel on the back. It almost made Daniel cry. Without saying a word, Jim had said something loud and clear. He understood.

His mother's comment changed Daniel's attitude. After he and Jim changed their clothes and began shooting baskets in the driveway before lunch, he didn't feel like smiling and talking, as he had right after church.

Maryann came out to read a magazine in the sun, and Jim asked her to shoot a few baskets with Dan for a while. She sighed when Jim tossed her the ball. Even though she pretended not to enjoy it, she wasn't a bad shot. Jim had taught her well.

"Wanna play a little one-on-one, champ?" she asked. But Daniel wasn't in the mood. She was shocked. Usually *he* always bugged *her* to play.

A few minutes later, Mrs. Bradford emerged from the house and walked through the garage, still wearing her apron. Daniel wondered why she didn't just call them to lunch from the doorway as usual. But she came right out into the middle of the driveway. Jim was a few steps behind.

"Daniel, take a walk with me," she said and went right past him toward the back yard. Daniel flipped the ball to Jim. He immediately bounced it to Maryann and went into an exaggerated defense against her.

She squealed in frustration as Jim kept slapping at the ball while she tried to get around him. Daniel followed his mother. The sounds of his brother and sister teasing each other in the driveway faded.

His mother slowed and let him catch up with her. She wiped her hands on her apron and reached up to put her arm around his shoulders. "Getting too big for this?" she asked.

He shook his head.

"I need to apologize to you, Dan," she said. "I'm sorry for what I said to you."

He didn't know what to say, so he said nothing.

"I was wrong, and I want you to forgive me. Will you?" she asked.

"Sure, Mom," he said quietly, not looking at her. "It's all right."

"No, it's not all right. I hurt you! I want that happy boy back, the one who was ready for church this morning and seemed to have a good time there. Is he back?"

Daniel shrugged.

"See?" she said. "It's not all right, is it? Mom's big mouth spoiled everything."

Daniel scowled. He wanted to be happy again. But his attitude *had* changed. He couldn't truthfully say she was wrong about that. But he forgave her. He had told her that. It's just that everything wasn't *all* better all of a sudden. And he couldn't pretend that it was.

Daniel stopped and gently pulled away. "Can I play basketball now, Mom?" he said.

"If you're sure everything is all right again," she said. "You were so happy this morning."

"I know," he said. "I still am. Only it's a little different now, that's all."

"Because of what I said?"

He shrugged. "I guess."

"I'm sorry."

"I *know*," he said. "It's all right."

"No, it isn't," she said. "I can tell. Talk to me, Daniel."

He leaned up against the corner of the house and stared at his feet. "I wasn't trying to fool you," he said. "I knew I couldn't watch TV today."

She nodded, staring intently at him.

"I was just really happy today. I don't know why."

"Yes, you do," she said, smiling. "Jim was right. You're excited about tomorrow."

She cupped his face in her hands and forced him to look into her eyes. "And I'm excited for you," she added. "I think it's going to be fun."

He couldn't resist a smile.

"And I also think you're wonderful," she said. She hugged him again.

He didn't hug her, but he didn't pull away either.

That afternoon Daniel lay on his bed and listened to the radio. Buck Spangler hit a home run, two singles, and batted in three runs in the first game. Daniel was happy again, but the time seemed to drag.

Even though evening church service caused him to miss the end of the second game, it also helped him pass the time. He enjoyed it as he had this morning. Everyone noticed again.

Daniel was amazed at how having something exciting to look forward to seemed to change the way he looked at everything. It didn't even bother him when he learned that Spangler had no hits in the second game of the double header, struck out twice, and made an error that lost the game.

He wished it had been different, of course. But it didn't seem to make all that much difference now. What mattered was tomorrow. The call to Mr. Epton. The drive to town. His first meeting with a new friend.

Who would it be? What would it be like to have someone his own age to play with, to talk to, to care about? Would he like them—would they like him? Would they be interested in the same things he was—like sports?

7

The Big Day

Daniel was up early Monday morning, reading the sports page and watching the clock. He wished his mother would get up. Of course, she couldn't call Mr. Epton until after eight, but Daniel could hardly wait.

His father came downstairs at about seven, and his mother a few minutes later. While she started breakfast, Daniel and his dad set the table. Then they went into the living room.

"Today's your big day, huh, Dan?"

"Yeah."

"Mine, too."

"Really? What're you doing, Dad?"

"Going back to Florida for a few days."

"You like that that much?"

"Oh, it gets to be a grind now and then. But we're testing a new piece of machinery this time. It's a plane that will fly in space as well as within our own atmosphere."

"Like the shuttle?"

"Sort of, but much more advanced. Some day this plane will take off from the ground, like any other jet, get up to full speed and altitude in a matter of minutes, and then be able to rocket into outer space from there."

"Wow! How can they do that?"

"That's what they're going to try to teach us this week. They want us to know how it works before we start flying around in it."

"Will you fly it into space, Dad?"

"Not this time. It's not really ready for that. Maybe next year. I'll get to fly this week, I think. By the time it's equipped to go into space, though, I may not be qualified to fly it into the second stage."

"What do you mean not qualified?"

"Well, to go into space I'd have to be an astronaut, not just a test pilot. That takes a lot more training and testing. And there are many men already qualified, years younger than I am, who would give anything for a space mission. I'd say it's unlikely I'll get a chance."

"Then why do they want you to fly the plane?"

Mr. Bradford laughed. "I'm the guinea pig," he said. "The test pilots get the dangerous part. If the plane holds up at high speeds—the way they think it will in our atmosphere—then they'll start adding equipment that will make it go into space."

Daniel thought for a moment. "You're in as good a shape as those younger guys, aren't you, Dad?"

Mr. Bradford smiled. "In the tests I always do pretty well," he said. "I usually finish among the top ten percent."

"Then I think you could be an astronaut, even if you are old."

"Hey! I'm not old! Just older! Anyway, Dan, don't count on it, and don't you tell anyone about it. You see, I would have to be in the top one or two percent to even be considered for a mission like that."

"Then how come you're so excited about flying that plane?"

"Just because I like new equipment. New challenges. New risks. And I also like to feel that I'm in on the ground floor of an exciting new project. You know what I mean?"

"Not really."

"When you watch television a few years from now, and see this self-contained jet and space capsule blast out of the earth's atmosphere, you'll know that your dad flew one of the first test missions. For now, I'll be doing my best to learn everything I can about the craft, so NASA will have all the information they need."

Daniel fell silent. He was proud of his father. But he thought it was unfair that Dad couldn't be the one who flew the craft into space, too. "Have you given up on being an astronaut?" he asked.

"Oh, no! If I'm given the chance to test it, I'll be ready. We always have to do that, Dan. But I'm just being realistic. If I get so excited about becoming an astronaut that I feel terrible if I don't become one, that would be bad. Especially, when I know that it's unlikely because of my age and all the other men who are shooting for the same goal."

Daniel nodded, but he was still confident that his dad could get one of the positions.

"There's a reason I told you all this, Dan," his dad said. "I want you to be realistic today, too."

"What do you mean?"

"I mean I know what you're thinking now. And I know what you'll be thinking when you play with those kids today. You're going to befriend somebody that you'll want to bring home. And you can't do that. We want you to do this, and enjoy yourself, and make new friends, and help out. But we don't want you setting your sights on a new brother or sister."

"I'm not—"

"I know you're not thinking that right now. But it'll happen. I'd rather see you do what I'm doing. Give it your best. Give it your all. Be satisfied with that. We are not in a position to care for any more children right now. Or adopt any, either."

"But you have plenty of money."

"Money isn't the point. We have our family. We have our plans."

"And we have plenty of room."

"I know that, Daniel. But I'm telling you that we are happy with our family just as it is. If you need more friends, you'll need to look for more opportunities like this one. You can have school friends over more, and kids from church. OK?"

Daniel didn't know what to say. Why was his dad spoiling this before it even got started? He knew his dad didn't mean to. But it made him feel the same way he had the day before when his mother accused him of acting good just to get to watch TV.

"OK," he muttered. He was noticing that the smells of breakfast had brought Jim and Maryann padding down to the table.

"I'm going to miss you this week," Mr. Bradford told him. "I'll probably see you Friday."

"I'm gonna miss you, too," Daniel said. Jim sat at the table in his lifeguard uniform: sandals, trunks, terrycloth top, whistle, and floppy cap with sunglasses attached. His mother pointed to the cap as she sat down. Jim swiped it off his head and put it beneath his chair.

Maryann looked pretty in a bright red outfit. She would be crafts supervisor in a playground program. "Are you going to feel lost without your car, hotshot?" she asked Jim.

"Don't get smart," he said, smiling, "or I'll change my mind."

Mrs. Bradford looked up. "Oh, Maryann gets the Camaro today, huh?" she said.

"Yeah," Jim said. "And everyday. She needs it more'n I do during the day. Anyway it would be a long way out of my way to drop her off and pick her up."

"So I'll drop *him* off and pick *him* up," Maryann said. "But ask him the real reason."

Everyone looked at Jim, who turned red. "Not fair," he said sheepishly.

"C'mon," Mr. Bradford said. "What'd you talk her into for the privilege of driving your car everyday?"

Jim pointed to Maryann to keep her from telling. "One word and I can change my mind," he said.

"I want to know," Mrs. Bradford said, laughing.

Jim swallowed a mouthful of food. "Ah, she's just gonna do some stuff for me. Clean my room, that kinda stuff."

"That's nice," his mother said. "Is that all? I can tell it isn't by the look on Maryann's face."

Maryann was fighting a grin and shaking her head.

"Not one word," Jim said. "You know you get to use the car for going to lunch and everything. Don't risk that."

Maryann wouldn't say anything.

Mr. Bradford cleared his throat and watched Jim carefully. "Jimbo," he said slowly, "what gives me the impression this concerns a young lady?"

Jim looked frustrated and embarrassed. Maryann burst into laughter. "I didn't say anything, Jim!" she said. "You know I didn't say anything!"

"And don't!" he said, unable to keep from smiling now himself.

"C'mon," his dad pushed. "What's her name? One of Maryann's friends?"

"You might as well tell him, Mar," Jim said. "He has a way of knowing everything anyway."

"And I still get to use the car?" she said.

"Of course."

"Patsy Stryker," Maryann said. "I pick her up before I drop Jim off at the pool. Later I drop her off at home after I pick up Jim. So both ways he rides part of the way with her."

Jim was embarrassed but enjoying it. Daniel was, too. But something about it made him sad. Fun like this between his brother and sister had been going on for years. He wasn't old enough to really be in on it. He knew that long after they were gone he'd sit at home with just his parents. And no one would be there to tease him and have fun with him.

They were lucky to have each other. So lucky.

8

A Bad Start

Just before nine, Daniel's mother let him listen on the extension phone as she called Mr. Epton at the children's home. Fortunately, Mr Epton sounded much warmer that Miss Simpson had.

"Yes, Mrs. Bradford, I got the message about your son Jimmy—"

"Daniel," she corrected.

"Oh, yes. Well, the note says James."

"That's my older son. He brought Daniel there—"

"I'm sorry, Mrs. Bradford. Anyway, we appreciate your son Daniel's interest. The fact is, the future of the home is shaky at best, and—"

"You mean you're about to be closed?" Mrs. Bradford asked.

"That's a very real possibility."

"Then why didn't your helper, Miss, ah, Simpson, tell my son that this program is no longer available?"

"I'm afraid Miss Simpson is not always up on the latest information, Mrs. Bradford. She is just a weekend employee. Now, the program is available as long as the home is open.

44

It's just that it seems a lot of trouble for you to drive in here, be interviewed, and fill out all these forms, when, in as little as a month or two, this place could be closed."

Mrs. Bradford paused before she spoke. Then she was very direct. "Have you found this program good for the children there?"

"Of course. More so to the visitors than to the visited, mind you, but, yes, of course."

"Then I think we'll just take our chances on the future of the home," she said.

"I look forward to meeting you this afternoon, Ma'am. And your son, of course."

Daniel did everything he could think of between the phone call and one o'clock, when he and his mother began to get ready for the drive into town. He rode his bicycle. He ran. He walked. He shot baskets. He tried to read, but he couldn't think. He even cleaned up his room.

His mother helped lug his ten-speed into the back of the station wagon. If she felt the route she drove was safe for riding his bike, she would leave the bike with him. Otherwise, she would just wait for him in the parking lot.

When they arrived at the home, she told him he could unload the bike and lock it into the bike rack. Inside, Mr. Epton was as nice as he had sounded on the phone. The balding man, with a pointy face and a bushy black mustache, had Daniel's mother fill out several forms and sign a few others. He gave her a brief tour. Then she kissed Daniel good-bye. He was embarrassed.

Mr. Epton spoke quickly when he was with Daniel alone. "Several of the children take turns showing outsiders the home. The boy assigned to you is Tony Rollo. Do you understand that he is assigned to you, not the other way around?"

"No, I don't understand."

"I mean that we make it appear that *you* are *his* responsibility, not the other way around. The children don't appreciate being assigned to someone from the outside who is expected to do them the favor of playing with them."

"I see."

"Tony is a pretty fast kid, so don't let him get you into trouble. If there is any trouble while you're here, you'll not be allowed back. OK?"

Daniel nodded, already wondering if this was all that he had built it up to be. He couldn't help but remember his dad's advice from that morning. He would just give it his best.

He had sort of hoped that he could watch the kids play a while and then choose one or two who looked especially lonely. But when Tony Rollo showed up, Daniel knew he would be playing by their rules.

Tom was a short, wiry kid with long dark hair and heavy eyebrows. His shirt tail hung out. His belt was much too large. His pants came to the tops of his ankles, and he wore two different colors of socks. He had sneakers on.

Daniel put out his hand. But Tony ignored it until Mr. Epton looked at him. Then he gripped it lightly and let it go quickly as he looked Daniel up and down. "Nice to meet you," he said. Daniel couldn't tell if he meant it or not.

Mr. Epton told Daniel that the hours between two and four weekday afternoons during the summer were free time for those who had finished all their chores, made their beds, and were not grounded.

"Tony here will show you the grounds. Then you can join in playing with any of the children you like. Right, Tony?"

"Yes, sir," Tony said without a smile. He motioned with his head that Daniel should follow him. He walked slowly out of the office, through the waiting area, down the wide dark corridor out of view of the front doors, and headed left down a narrow hallway.

Just before they made the turn, Daniel felt uncomfortable. Tony hadn't spoken since they left Mr. Epton's office. "Thanks for showing me around," Daniel said weakly.

Tony slowed nearly to a stop. He stared at Daniel and

shook his head as if he was very angry at this outsider. Without warning he took off running. The hall was a scary, echoing cave of a place, made of hardwood floors and dark wood walls and doors.

Tony was twenty feet away by the time Daniel realized that he would have to run full speed to stay close. Their shoes made a deafening clatter in the hall. Daniel squinted to see where he was going. Tony turned right at the end of the hall. Just as Daniel slowed a bit to make the turn, he heard a woman shout from the other end, "No running! Stop that running, boys!"

Daniel stopped, almost glad to know there was an adult nearby. But as he turned to look back, Tony reappeared. He grabbed him by the shirt and pulled him around the corner. Breaking away from him, Tony began running fast again.

Daniel hesitated, then started running again himself. He didn't want to break the rules. But they were already getting into some dark passageways where only Tony could find the way. Daniel didn't want to get lost or lag behind and be punished for causing all the noise.

For a second he could hear Tony's pounding footsteps. But he had lost sight of him. When he got to the next corner where two hallways met, he slowed and walked cautiously, squinting to try to see Tony.

He looked to the left. But Tony grabbed him from the right and slammed him up against the wall. "Here's how it works," Tony said, hissing in Daniel's face. "I know you were forced to come here just like I was forced to show you around. Only I'm not showing you around. You don't want to see this place any more'n I wanna show it to you."

He pointed to his left. "That way is the gym and the game rooms." He pointed to his right. "That way is the dorms and the classrooms. There's a playground in the middle courtyard straight ahead. You do what you want and go where you want. If anyone asks you about me, you tell 'em I'll be right back. We meet back here, right here, at four. I'll walk you back to Epton's office. You tell 'em how nice I was.

I'll tell 'im how good it was to have you here. Deal?"

Daniel started to protest. He wanted to tell Tony that he had wanted to come, that he wasn't forced. He wanted to tell him also that he couldn't lie for him or anything like that. But Tony had run off. Daniel followed him for a few steps, until Tony burst through the doors to the playground.

Daniel watched through the window for a few minutes. He saw Tony join five or six other boys about his age and size. They roamed the playground and took toys from the other kids, flinging them away so that the younger or smaller ones had to go get them.

They dragged kids out of the swings. But then they lost interest in swinging themselves and moved on to other mischief. Most of the children just cleared a path when the bullies came through. When any of the workers appeared, Tony and his friends just huddled to talk until the danger cleared.

Daniel wanted to run back to Mr. Epton's office and tell on Tony and his friends. Then he wanted to ride home as fast as he could. He wanted to tell his mother that he was happy with his family just the way it was.

He started to run. But then his father's advice came to his mind. He slowed to a walk and then stopped. He knew what he had to do. He had to make friends with someone who needed a friend. He had to give it his best shot. He had to give it his all.

9

Yo-Yo, the Storyteller

Daniel made his way carefully down the corridor to the dorms and classrooms. He realized that the whole complex seemed to be made up of the same type of huge, dark, old-fashioned buildings.

There was lots of color. But there were hardly any windows because the buildings were so old. He peeked into a few of the larger rooms and guessed that these were where a few privileged kids slept. A couple of the rooms had eight double bunk beds each. From the things tacked on the walls, it was clear that the room was for junior-high girls.

Two turns and several steps later, Daniel found a wing that obviously housed boys of all ages. There was one huge room with at least a hundred beds. There were a few smaller rooms like the ones he had seen in the girl's wing.

A half dozen kids lay on their cots, reading or sleeping or humming. One was crying. Daniel went toward him, but, as he got near, the little guy turned toward the wall. Daniel felt like crying, too. He wondered how long the boy had been in the home.

When he moved out into the hallway again, an adult

worker eyed him carefully. "You new here, son?" the man said kindly.

"No, sir," Daniel said, surprising himself at how hard it was to speak normally. "Just visiting."

"Who's your host?"

"My host?"

"Your guide, son. I think maybe you'd better come with me. I'm fairly new here myself. If you're a visitor, Mr. Epton will know. No one from the outside should be in here without a guide."

"Oh, my guide. Yes, sir, my guide. That would be Tony, sir. Tony Rollo, yes, sir."

The man cocked his head and studied Daniel. "Tony? Where is he?"

"We're meeting in a little while, sir. He'll be back."

"Where're you meeting him?"

"Down the hall in the other wing there."

The man nodded and walked away. Daniel could breathe again. He headed toward the other side of the complex, past the playground area, and into the game rooms. On his way past the exit to the playground, he stopped and peeped out again.

Tony and his buddies were still bothering the younger, smaller kids. But there was no fighting. Everyone was either afraid of the bullies, or they had tried to get them in trouble before and failed.

Daniel was fascinated at the scene in one of the game rooms. It was cool, air conditioned, even with the sun high in the sky outside. In the huge room fifty or sixty children, in little groups of five or six, played noisy games.

A matron sat near the door, almost like a schoolteacher, watching the children. Often one would come up and ask her something or tell her something. The woman smiled at them and gave them her full attention.

Daniel stood in the doorway looking past her for several minutes until she noticed him. He asked if he could just go in and watch the kids play. She smiled and nodded.

Many of the kids, especially the younger girls, seemed to want her to look at them and talk to them. Daniel hoped he looked old enough for the kids to come and talk to him, too.

Then it hit him. This wasn't just a game room for the ones who didn't want to be outside. This was for the younger kids. He didn't see any he thought were even his own age. One or two of the boys might have been nine.

Several were playing with toy musical instruments. Some were throwing bean bags. Some were using glue and crayons or playing with blocks, clay, or stuffed animals.

Some of the noise, but not very much, died down. Dozens of pairs of little eyes followed Daniel as he moved into the center of the room.

He had not expected to see the very, very young children, some even preschool age. But both boys and girls came up to him, reached out to him, touched him, grasped him around the legs, and walked along with him.

One little black girl looked up into his face and held out her arms as if she wanted him to hold her. He would have, too, except so many children crowded around him that he couldn't get to her.

Daniel put his hands on a couple of the kid's shoulders as he walked to a chair and sat down. As soon as he was settled, three children climbed into his lap. They didn't say anything. They just looked into his eyes as if they wanted him to look into their eyes.

And so he did. He smiled at them. They looked away shyly, looking back at him again as soon as they saw him turn away. It seemed they were hungry for any attention. So he gave it to them. He wanted to talk to them, to say something to make them know what he was feeling.

But he didn't know what to say. He felt, if he really opened his mouth and tried to speak, he would cry. He didn't know why. This was really bothering him. It was like nothing he had expected. He didn't know what to think about it.

Four children were holding hands all at the same time,

squeezing his fingers. They were running their hands up and down his arms. He tickled a couple. They giggled and ran away, only to come back for more.

He wanted to see what else was going on in the room, so he stood again. The ones on his lap tried to hang on. They almost fell as he stood, but he let them down gently. He walked to another table and chair in the back of the room. But most of the kids stayed right with him.

As he reached the chair, he saw a group of about twelve children sitting around a dark haired girl whose back was to him. He was amazed. It appeared that this tiny one was teaching the others or telling them a story.

He stared at the group until the ones climbing on him drifted away, back to their toys. They had probably wanted hugs and kisses. But Daniel wasn't ready for that, and he felt that maybe he shouldn't do it.

Now he sat alone in the back corner of the noisy, crowded room, not far from the small circle of boys and girls— none of them older than seven, except perhaps their little storyteller.

She was not much bigger than they were. Daniel couldn't quite hear what she was saying. She was so good at holding their attention, however, that he knew she had to be at least nine or ten. He slid his chair closer, still facing the back of the little leader. Not one of the children noticed him, certainly not the leader. She moved her arms and hands as she spoke and used her voice to show drama or emotion.

Daniel strained to hear her. He didn't want to bother her or any of her listeners. But he just had to know what she was saying that kept their attention so well.

She was telling a story, a beautiful story. It was about an orphan whose parents had to leave her in the care of the police because they couldn't afford to keep her anymore. The police placed her in an orphanage where she was very sad and lonely for many years.

She felt mistreated and had few friends. Every night she prayed that someone would adopt her and make her part of his family. Finally, the big day came, the little storyteller said, "And Amy was adopted by a young couple who didn't have any other children.

"Her new mommy and daddy put her in their car and drove to their little house in the country. Then they discovered that she was the same little baby they had given to the police many years before."

Daniel was almost in tears. The girl who told the story had almost cried herself. The children loved the story. And it seemed to Daniel that they had probably heard it many times before.

"Tell it again, Yo-Yo," they begged.

"That *was* a beautiful story," Daniel said, causing several of the children to jump and the little storyteller to turn around. She was tiny, but her huge, almost black, eyes couldn't hide a sadness that came with more years than her little body showed.

She had long, pitch-black hair, and deep bronze skin. She looked Mexican to Daniel. When she smiled, with large, perfect, gleaming teeth, he thought she was the most beautiful little girl he had ever seen.

He would ask her why they called her Yo-Yo, as soon as he was able to speak.

10

Threatening Tony Rollo

"And what's your name?" asked the dark little girl the other kids called Yo-Yo.

"Dan," was all Daniel could manage.

"And do you have a last name, Dan?" she asked. She was walking away from the other kids, leading him to a far corner of the room.

"Bradford," he said, not taking his eyes off her. She put out her hand and shook his.

"Welcome to the home."

"I'm just a visitor," he said.

"That's what I thought," she said. "And your host ditched you, didn't he?"

Daniel couldn't believe how friendly this girl was. He nodded to answer her question.

"Tell me where you're supposed to meet him, and I'll guess which one he is."

Daniel fumbled for the words.

"If it's near the front lobby, that would be Dwayne," she said. But she could tell by the look on Daniel's face that his host was not Dwayne. "Then Willie or Tony," she said. "Let me guess. Um, Willie!"

"Nope," he said, and she laughed loudly.

"Oh, Tony then!" she said, punching the air but still smiling. "I missed it, didn't I?"

Daniel nodded. What a precious girl this was. "How old are you?" he asked.

"Just turned ten," she said.

"Happy birthday, Yo-Yo," Daniel said. She suddenly turned very serious. He was afraid he had said something wrong. "Shouldn't I call you Yo-Yo?" he asked. "That's your nickname, isn't it?"

"Oh, that's all right," she said. "It's just that you're the only person outside of here who wished me happy birthday."

Daniel scowled. "Nobody sent you anything?"

"I got a package from the home. The same one everyone gets. It has a comb and a brush and a candy bar and an apple. I saved it until the apple was rotten. I pretended it came from my mom and dad."

Daniel didn't know what to say. "Why do they call you Yo-Yo?" he asked finally.

"It's from the first part of my first name and the last part of my last name. Can you guess my names?"

He thought for a moment. He couldn't think of any girl names that started with a Yo sound. He shrugged.

"Give up?" she asked, smiling playfully again.

"Yolanda Trevino. You say it like Tre-veen-yo. See? Yo-Yo."

"Do you like being called Yo-Yo?"

"Sure. It's different."

"But if everyone calls you Yo-Yo, it's not different anymore."

"What would you like to call me, Dan?"

"I'll call you Yolanda. And you call me Daniel, OK?"

"OK, Daniel. You want me to help you stay out of trouble with Tony?"

"Sure."

"Then don't meet him at four o'clock. Go with me to the office and tell Mr. Epton that you lost track of Tony. Tell him that you would rather have me be your hostess. Then if Tony wants to lie to get out of it, that's his problem, not yours."

"But I want to come here everyday and try to make friends with some of the children," Daniel said. "Are you sure you want to be my hostess everyday?"

"After a while you won't need anyone to show you around. But until then, it will be all right. I'll enjoy it, I think."

She took Daniel's hand and led him up to the matron at the front of the room. "We're going to the office, Miss Melody," Yolanda said. "I'll be back soon."

Miss Melody winked at her.

"You *lost* him somewhere?" Mr. Epton repeated.

"Sort of, sir. Actually, he said he'd meet me just before four o'clock, and we'd come back here together."

"He *planned* this? I mean, he, he—"

"Tony ditched him," Yolanda said sweetly. "But I'll be happy to be his hostess until he knows his way around here."

But Mr. Epton wasn't listening. He called his secretary on the intercom. "Have Tony Rollo paged and get him in here right away," he said.

He looked up and noticed that Daniel and Yolanda were still standing there. He spoke gently. "You take care of him until four o'clock," he told Yolanda. "Then bring him back here."

They were walking back toward the game room when Tony came hurrying toward the office. He hardly noticed them at first. Then he stopped. "You!" he said, pointing at Yolanda. "You squealed on me? Is that why old man Epton wants to see me?"

Daniel froze as Tony came up to them.

"Yes, I did," Yolanda said simply.

Tony glared at her. "You again, Yo-Yo?"

She nodded. "I'm not going to quit telling on you, Tony, as long as you keep doing this. It isn't nice. It isn't right. It isn't fair."

"I didn't convince you last time, huh?" Tony said. "Maybe I'll use a little help from my friends this time. You're gonna be sorry, you little Mex. Take my word for it."

Yolanda's lip quivered. But she looked more hurt than scared. Something was welling up in Daniel that he couldn't control. His breath came in short gasps through his nose and his chest heaved. Yolanda dropped her head and kept walking. But Daniel turned toward the office.

"Hey!" Daniel shouted, almost screaming. It made both Tony and Yolanda jump. Tony looked back without stopping. "I'm talking to you, Tony!" Daniel yelled. Tony stopped.

Daniel's face was red. He pointed at Tony down the hall. "Anything happens to this girl," he shouted, "no matter if you do it or your friends do it, I'm comin' after you!"

Tony waved disgustedly at him, as if to brush him off. Suddenly Daniel found himself racing down the hallway. He skidded to a stop in front of Tony before he had a chance to move.

"You don't believe me?" Daniel said, putting his face up next to Tony's.

"Ah," Tony said. He sneered at Daniel and started to walk away.

Daniel had never touched anyone in anger, but he grabbed Tony's shoulder and wheeled him around to face him. He pushed Tony back up against the wall. "I want to know that you heard me, Tony," Daniel said. "I want to know that you understand me."

Tony just glared at him.

"I'm telling you that you will have to answer to me if anybody touches Yolanda. You got that?"

Tony tried to pull away. But Daniel held him tight against the wall. "You got that?" he demanded.

"All right, all right!" Tony shouted. And he ran away.

Daniel was shaking as he returned to Yolanda. He didn't know what had come over him. He knew it wasn't right to fight. And he hated to think of what he would have to do if something *did* happen to Yolanda. He had threatened Tony, and he would have to do something. One thing he knew for sure: it was right to protect someone. And for some reason, he wanted to protect this little girl.

Little girl? She wasn't even two years younger than he was. But there was something special about her. They had known each other for only a few minutes, yet they had stuck up for each other already.

Yolanda was silent as they walked back to the game room. Daniel wondered if she was crying. But he didn't want to embarrass her by looking at her closely enough to see. "What did Tony do to you last time?" he asked.

She stopped and covered her face with her hands and cried softly. Daniel felt terrible. He wanted to put his hands on her shoulder and comfort her, but he didn't dare. He remembered how good it felt when his brother had comforted him in the car the day before, but he just couldn't bring himself to do it.

How could anyone have hurt this sweet girl? he wondered. Daniel just stood looking at his feet as she cried. Finally, she spoke softly.

"It was more than a month ago. I got him in trouble for doing to someone else the same thing he did to you today. He told me he was going to punch me in the mouth. I was afraid for a while, but then I just forgot about it.

"He got into our dorm room one night. I woke up just before he hit me—just in time to see something coming toward my face. I didn't even have time to move. It felt like he hit me on the mouth with a book or something like that. I screamed and someone turned the lights on. But he was gone."

"Did they catch him?"

"No. And I couldn't prove it was him. I told them that he had promised to hit me in the mouth. But he said he didn't do it. So what could they do?"

"Were you hurt bad?"

"Two stitches."

"Really? Where?"

She pulled her hands away from her face and showed him a small crease in her upper lip.

"You can't tell," he said. "I mean I never would have noticed."

"That's what the doctor promised me," she said, smiling weakly. "He said children's lips heal fast." And that made her laugh.

Daniel laughed too.

They went back to the game room and sat at a table near the back. And for the next hour and a half they told each other about themselves.

11
The Phone Call

Daniel raced all the way home at top speed. Yet, when he parked his bike in the garage, he wasn't breathing hard. From the time he got in the back door, until after Jim and Maryann got home, he talked nonstop about the home and especially about Yolanda Trevino. He was still talking at the dinner table.

"Yo-Yo," Maryann said, smiling. "What a cute nickname."

"But I'm not going to call her that," Daniel announced. "Everyone calls her that. I think she'd like for me to call her by her real name. She never knew her mom and dad. They were killed in a car crash when she was a baby. She was staying with her aunt in Texas. Her parents were the kind of farmers that travel around and pick crops for other people."

"Migrant workers," Jim said.

"Yeah. Anyway, when her parents died, her aunt just kept Yolanda in her family. But she already had a bunch of kids. And her husband was bad."

"What do you mean by bad?" Mrs. Bradford asked.

"He drinks a lot. And he isn't home very much. And he

60

spanks the kids too hard—and even fights with his wife."

"You mean he actually fights with her?" Jim asked.

"Yes! That's why Yolanda's aunt sent her to a home. This is the third one she's been in. Her aunt hasn't come to see her—or even written to her since the first one."

"Maybe her aunt has lost track of her," Daniel's mother suggested.

"Nope. She knows where Yolanda is. She just doesn't want to have anything more to do with her. But I don't think it's because she doesn't care."

Maryann put down her fork. "Then why would she quit writing to her niece?"

"Her husband won't let her. When the first home closed, Yolanda went back with her aunt and uncle for a little while. He beat her. She doesn't want to go back there again. But she would like to hear from her aunt now and then."

Maryann left the table in tears.

"How sad," Mrs. Bradford said. "How terribly sad."

Jim just shook his head.

"Can I call her tonight, Mom?" Daniel asked.

"Call her?"

"Yeah. She said she never gets any phone calls, like some of the other kids do."

"I don't know, Daniel. How would you be sure to catch her when she's not at dinner or some other activity?"

"I checked the schedule. I know just when to call."

"Is she expecting you to call? Don't start promising her things when you might have to disappoint her."

"No! This would be a surprise."

"I'll think about it," his mother said. "First, you have some jobs to do around here. And then I think you ought to remember to pray for that boy who threatened her."

Daniel had told them everything about Tony, except the part where he threatened *him*.

"I will, Mom," he promised. "Then can I call her? Just to say hi, so she can have a phone call?"

"How long will you talk?"

"It won't take long to say hi. Anyway, I wouldn't know what else to say. Could I put you on, and maybe Jim and Maryann, so you could all meet her over the phone?"

"No," Mrs. Bradford said. "We'll get a chance to meet her someday."

Maryann had just returned to the table. "*I'll* meet her over the phone, Mom! I think that's a great idea. Let's do it."

"You can if you want to," Mom said. "I prefer to meet her in person sometime. Maybe in a few weeks. She *does* sound like a wonderful little girl."

Daniel smiled.

Daniel and Maryann had a very brief chat with Yolanda about seven o'clock. Actually, Maryann and Yolanda talked much longer than Daniel and Yolanda did. Daniel couldn't think of anything to say.

Yolanda was thrilled to get her first-ever phone call at the home. The next day she told Daniel that everyone had asked her about it. That night when Daniel's dad called from Florida, Daniel got on and told him the whole story.

"I'm glad to hear you're making friends, Daniel," Dad said. "After I get back, I'll go over there and meet a few of them myself. I think it would be interesting."

By Friday, the home was all Daniel cared about, thought about, or talked about. Maryann had driven over on Thursday during an afternoon break. Daniel had showed her around.

He had even introduced her to Tony, hoping that Tony would be nice and that maybe they would not have to be mean to each other anymore. Tony watched as Daniel and Maryann attached his ten-speed to the bike rack on the back of Jim's Camaro.

Maryann drove Daniel home before heading back to work. They had a good chance to talk. "I think this is good for you, Dan," she said.

"I know it is."

"I remember your first reaction to the home," she said. "Scary, you said. You just wanted to get out. It had made me

62

sad. I pitied those kids. I'll bet that's how you feel now, too."

"Sort of, Maryann," Daniel admitted. "But you know, not even someone like Yolanda actually wants to be pitied. I think what they want more than anything else in the world—if they can't be part of a family—is to be treated like normal people."

"Is that what you do, Dan?" Maryann asked. "Do you treat them like normal people?"

"I treat them like brothers and sisters," he said.

"Oh, I hope you don't treat them like you treat me!" she kidded. He laughed. "Even Yolanda?" she added.

"Especially Yolanda. I pretend she's my little sister. She pretends I'm her big brother. There's something unusual about her, though, Maryann."

"I know. She's special."

"Yeah, but there's more. Did you know that almost all the little girls there treat her like she's their older sister? Some even treat her like she's their mom. She's good at it, too. She tells them stories. Takes care of them. Helps when they're sad or tired or lonely."

"That's sweet."

"Yeah, but she doesn't have anyone to go to herself."

"She has you, Dan."

"I know, but I don't spend all my time with her. There are some guys I play with. And lots of other kids to talk to. Anyway, I'm only there a couple of hours a day. She needs someone she can look up to and talk to. Someone she can use as a big sister."

Maryann pulled into the driveway. She quickly helped Daniel unload his bike. "I've got to run," she said. "You almost made me think I ought to move into the home and be Yolanda's big sister."

"You'd be a good one, Maryann," Daniel said, smiling.

"What do you mean, would be?" she asked, getting back into the car. "I already am one! You know what, though, Dan? You have something I don't have."

"What's that?"

"A sister."

She looked into Daniel's eyes as it sank in. "You're right," he said, as she pulled away. "I never thought of that."

It was good to have his father home that weekend. Daniel spent a lot of time telling him about all his experiences at the home. He pleaded with his father to see about having some of the kids out to the house. His father, as usual, said maybe.

It was on Monday, two weeks later, when trouble struck. Double trouble.

First, when Daniel arrived at the home, the kids were strangely quiet. There were always plenty of children who were sad or seemed lonely. That was only natural. But this day it was different. It was everybody.

Not even Yolanda seemed like herself. She seemed to be thinking about something else all the time. When Tony saw Daniel, he didn't even glare at him or say anything. He just ignored him. After about an hour of trying to play with several kids, Daniel pulled Yolanda off to the side.

"What's the deal?" he asked. "I've been coming here for three weeks, and I thought I was everyone's friend. Everyone except Tony and his buddies, of course. But no one will tell me what's wrong."

In her excited, earnest way, Yolanda told him. There had been an announcement. The home was going to be closed in six weeks. Money from the state had been cut, and, besides, the place was too old and too big for the number of children that were there. They would all be moving again.

12
Tony's Confession

"Where?" Daniel asked, a lump in his throat.

"We never know," she said. "We'll probably all go different places."

He sat with his head in his hands, wondering what it all meant. "That's why everyone's being very quiet, even with each other?"

She nodded. "We're starting to say good-bye now, just in case. We can't stay too close to even our best friends, because we may never see them again after next month."

She started to cry. But when she noticed some of her friends looking, she quickly smiled at them. Daniel shook his head. How could she do it? She was so tiny, so weak looking. Yet she was stronger than he was. She had not been afraid of Tony. She would not cry in front of the little ones. She would be brave.

"Does that mean you'll treat me differently, too?" Daniel asked.

"Probably," she said simply. "I'll miss you. I don't like good-byes."

She couldn't say any more.

"So you want me to stop coming to see you and the others?" he asked.

She pressed her lips together tightly to keep from crying. She nodded silently. "Maybe," she whispered.

Daniel hadn't been ready for that answer. Was she just trying to be strong? Did she mean it? Could his new world have started to fall apart already—in one day?

"I'll see you tomorrow, at least," he said, getting up to leave. She nodded and walked outside with him.

He trudged to the bike rack and unlocked the combination chain. He didn't notice anything wrong until he tried to roll the bike back out of the slot. The wheels wouldn't turn. The brick that had smashed both front and back spokes still lay near the bike. The tires had been pulled away from the rim and were flat. One pedal had been bent. Daniel was scared. But he wasn't mad. He just went to the office and asked to use the phone to call home for a ride.

Daniel sat down on the bike rack to wait. He tried to pray. Half an hour later, his father drove up. "Do you know who did this, Dan?" he asked gently.

"I have a pretty good idea," Daniel said. "It's the kid I've been praying for for weeks—Tony!"

His father silently put the bike into the back of the station wagon. Daniel slid into the front seat, and the tears came. "I don't understand it, Dad! I prayed for my enemy the way you and Mom said. I was worried more about what he'd do to Yolanda than what he might do to me. Last week there was a rumor that he and his buddies were going to jump me sometime. But I never gave them the chance."

Daniel broke the news about the closing of the home, and they rode the rest of the way in silence. Daniel's dad wasn't the kind who tried to always have an answer for everything, especially when there was no easy answer. Daniel was grateful for that.

When they stopped in the driveway, Mr. Bradford turned off the engine. But he didn't get out of the car. "Dan," he said, "we don't always understand how God works. All we can do is trust Him and believe that He knows best. I know that's not easy to take. And I can't promise just when we'll know what's good about this disappointment. But I know someday it will come."

Daniel was mad. Mad at God. He didn't want to admit that to his father. He didn't even want to admit it to God. He decided to give God one more chance.

"You know what I'm going to do, Dad?" he asked, crying. "I'm going to pray my hardest that Yolanda will get adopted before that place closes."

"Now, Daniel," his dad said, trying to soothe him, "that's not very long from now."

"I don't care! If I can't see her and pretend to be her brother, at least someone should be able to take her into their family. She tries so hard to be strong and brave in front of the smaller ones. But I know she just won't be able to take moving again."

Mr. Bradford could see that Daniel was not in the mood for advice, so he was quiet once more. Dan missed dinner that night and went to bed early. In the morning, he asked his mother if she would drive him to the home everyday until his bike got fixed.

To his surprise, she agreed immediately.

"Maybe Maryann can pick me up on the way home," he said.

"No, that's way out of her way," his mother said. "I'll either wait for you or come back for you. It's all right. I know how much it means to you to visit the children."

"I don't think the kids want me coming much longer, anyway," he said. "If I keep coming right up until their last day, it'll just make it harder when they all leave."

For the next several days, Daniel got sadder and sadder with each trip to the home. "Yolanda asked me today what I was going to do about Tony," he told his mother.

"And what did you say?"

"I said I was going to do nothing except treat him nice."

"Are you really going to?"

"I'm going to try. If he had hurt Yolanda, he would have been in big trouble with me. But since he took it out on me, I'm trying this way."

"You know that's what God would want you to do, don't you? To treat your enemies nice?"

Daniel wasn't in the mood to hear it. "Yeah," he muttered, "I guess. Only I'm not doing it as much for God or Tony as I am for Yolanda."

"Oh?"

"It's the way she treats people. And even if it isn't, she should see what happens when somebody treats a bully that way."

Within a week, Daniel found out how his experiment had worked. He was playing with a couple of young boys on the playground when Yolanda came running up. She was jumping and bubbling.

"Great news!" she said, flashing her biggest smile. "In fact, two good things!"

"What? What?" Daniel begged.

"Which one do you want to hear first?"

"How should I know?" Daniel asked. "I don't know which is best!"

"OK, I'll save the best until last. First, Tony is looking for you."

"That's *good* news?" Daniel said.

"Yes! He told me he was sorry about hitting me that time. And he said he had to apologize to you about something, too."

"Really?"

"Really! Something's really happened to him. Here he comes! See ya!"

She ran off, and Daniel stood as Tony approached. He couldn't tell if Tony was happy or sad or mad or just nervous.

"Can I talk to you for a minute?" Tony asked.

"Sure," Daniel said, walking with him.

"I wrecked your bike, and I'm sorry. I want to pay for

it," he said quickly. "You don't have to like me or be my friend, but I just want to do that."

Daniel looked at him. It was obvious that it had been very hard for Tony to say those things. Daniel stuck out his hand, and Tony shook it quickly.

"Why?" Daniel said.

"Why did I do it, or why am I sorry?"

"I know why you did it," Daniel said. "Because I threatened you."

"No, that's not it at all, man! I just hated you coming in here all rich and everything. I've seen you in two different cars, and I'll bet your dad has his own car, too."

Daniel started to nod but decided not to.

"And you've got that fancy bike and all the clothes and stuff you want. And you come and go in here all you want. And the little kids like you and look up to you."

Daniel didn't know what to say. He was starting to see why things would bother a kid like Tony. He wanted the kids to look up to him the way they looked up to Yolanda. That must have been why he hit her, too.

"But you've been nice to me. And to my little brother," Tony continued.

"Your little brother!"

"Yeah, Gino. The one you tell stories to—and take down the hallway when he's afraid to go alone."

"That's your brother? I didn't know that. He never says anything, so I guess he *wouldn't* tell me."

"I knew you didn't know. I also know it's not your fault you're rich. I know you're an OK guy."

"Hey, we're not rich," Daniel said.

Tony glared at him. "Don't tell *me* who's rich and who isn't," he said. "It doesn't take much to have more than we do."

Daniel couldn't argue with that. "You don't have to pay for the bike," he said. "My dad's having it fixed."

"There you go again, Dan," Tony said. "I need to pay you for that bike, don't you see? I know your family can handle it, so don't rub that in. We're going to be moving away from here soon, but I'm going to send you some money every month until we're even. And I want you to tell me exactly how much it costs to fix it. OK?"

"You really don't have—"

"Promise me, Daniel. I mean it."

"You don't have to pay for *all* of it—"

"I'm payin' for all of it and that's that," Tony said. "Will you promise to let me see the bill? Or do I have to beat it out of you?"

They both laughed and shook hands again. "It's a deal," Daniel said. "If you're sure."

"You say that one more time, and I'm gonna pop you one, Moneybags."

Tony ran off. Daniel felt as if he were floating. He had to find Yolanda. If she had more good news, and it was better than Tony's, he wanted to hear it.

13
Daniel's Big Surprise

When Daniel found Yolanda, it reminded him of the first time he had seen her. She was in a corner of the playground with a crowd around her, all listening.

He smiled as he walked up to them. But, just like the first time, no one even noticed him—least of all Yolanda. She was waving her arms. Her little voice was rising and falling as she told her story.

"The mother is pretty. And she asked a lot of good questions," she was saying. "The dad was kind of quiet, but he smiled at me a lot. I don't know where they live, and they wouldn't say their name. I'm not supposed to say anything about it, because parents usually talk to lots of children. But these people want a girl."

"Did they talk to any other girls, Yo-Yo?"

"Oh, I'm sure they did. But I didn't see any others while I was in there. I shouldn't say anything, but I really think they're going to take me."

There were squeals of delight and jumping and hugs as the other girls wished her well. "Wait!" she said. "Wait! You just can't say anything to anyone. It takes a long time, and who knows? It may never happen. I've been talked to before. Not too many times, but, still, it's never worked out."

"You never told us," someone said.

"That's because I could tell it wasn't going to happen. This time, I think it *is* going to happen."

Daniel waited off to the side until the little group broke up. "Hi, Yolanda," he said.

"Oh, Daniel, I wanted to tell you first. But I couldn't find you! I'm sorry."

"Don't be sorry. I'm happy for you."

"You don't look it."

"Don't I? I guess I don't know what I feel. It's what I wanted. It's what I've been praying for. That and for Tony. Looks like I got answers to both on the same day, huh?"

"Yeah. So smile."

But Daniel couldn't. He didn't know what was wrong.

"C'mon, big brother! It means I'll live close by, probably. You can come and see me! Who knows where they might have sent me?"

"Don't get your hopes too high, Yolanda. You know how these things go."

"Yeah. You think talking about it will jinx it?"

"I don't believe in jinxes. But I wouldn't tell anyone else. It'll probably be all over the home when your little friends are finished."

"Oh, no, they're good about keeping secrets. They really are. Of course, I told more of them this time, didn't I?" Daniel nodded. "And a few I didn't even know." Daniel nodded again. "Oh, boy."

"Well, don't worry about it," he said. "You can't change it now. When will you know if they take you or not?"

"I don't know. No one told me. They just said that by the time parents talk to kids they've already been checked out. Whatever that means."

"I guess it means making sure they have enough money, room, and are normal people, and everything," Daniel said.

"I guess," she said. Yo-Yo ran her fingers through her long, black hair. "I wish you'd act happier, Daniel."

"I'm trying."

"You're making me feel sad."

"Don't be sad. This will be the best thing that ever happened to you."

"Then why don't you smile about it?"

Daniel shook his head. He didn't know if he could talk without crying. "I don't know, Yolanda," he said. "I think maybe I didn't really think it would happen."

"Didn't you want it to happen?"

"Sure! Yeah! I've been praying for it. And I thought I was ready for it. But I guess I'm not."

"What do you mean, Daniel? You mean you would be happier if I didn't get adopted? If I was moved to some other home, away from you and all my friends—to somewhere I've never been?"

"No," he said miserably. "I guess it's just that if my family couldn't adopt you, I didn't want anyone to have you."

"*Your* family?"

"Sure. Both my mom and dad told me straight out that I shouldn't even ask. They said it long before I even started coming here. In fact, they thought my coming here and making friends would get me off my kick about them adopting me a brother or a sister."

Yolanda smiled sadly at Daniel. She understood what he was saying. She nodded and her smile faded. "Well, that's nice, I think," she said.

"It's nice?"

"Uh-huh. I mean, it's nice that you were really hoping I'd join your family. I never thought about that, because you have a brother and a sister. Right?"

"Right."

"Maybe I'm going to someone who doesn't have any children. And I'll mean as much to them as they do to me."

Daniel thought about that one for a minute. He knew she was right—even though she would mean every bit as much to his family, if they really got to know her.

"The thing is," he said, "I thought I had accepted it. I knew we couldn't have you, or anyone, and so I prayed that someone else would take you. Now they probably will. But it makes me feel sad, I guess. Like I'm losing you."

"That's sweet, Daniel. But don't you see? If this doesn't happen, we've lost each other."

Daniel looked at the ground. "I know you're right," he said. "And I know this is best—I really do. It's just that I can't smile about it yet. OK?"

Yolanda tried to smile for him. But she was sad now, too. "I think I know what you mean," she said. "When it happens, you'll get used to it. And you'll be happier than you would be if I had moved away from here."

Daniel sighed. "That's for sure. That would *really* make me sad." He didn't want to say any more, because he was about to cry. He waved good-bye to Yolanda and just walked away, through the double doors into the corridor. He went down the long dark hall and out through the front lobby to the curb.

The sun was hot. He moved over behind a corner of the building to wait for his mother to pick him up. He was out of sight, so he leaned against the building and let the tears come. He asked God why the answers to his prayers didn't make him happier.

He didn't feel as if God answered that question. And he knew why. Because he already knew the answer. His wish and hope had been that somehow, someway, his mom and dad would change their mind about adopting. He had convinced himself that it wouldn't happen. So he thought he had accepted it.

But he hadn't. It hurt. Knowing that Yolanda could, any day, join someone else's family, ended his hope. Even if he changed his parents' minds now, it was too late to adopt her.

Daniel was sure that whoever had interviewed Yolanda

would take her. No one who ever met Yolanda could forget her.

He wiped his eyes and folded his arms across his chest. He wanted to be happy for Yolanda. That would be his next project. He knew she was right. He knew it was better. He knew his parents' decision. So as soon as he could get over this disappointment, he was going to work up a smile for her and mean it.

As he stood there, he noticed his father's car in the parking lot. Puzzled, he walked over toward it. As he got near, he saw his parents coming from the building. "Mom! Dad! What are you doing here?"

His dad waved. "Your bike is finished," his dad said. "I thought you might want to ride it home. I've got it in the truck here. Where've you been? We were looking for you."

"I was just waiting for Mom," Daniel said. "I felt like leaving a little early today, that's all. Hey, you have to tell me how much the repairs cost, because the guy who did it admitted it today and wants to pay for it."

"Really?" Mrs. Bradford said. "That's wonderful! See how the Lord works?"

Daniel wasn't sure how the Lord had worked. He didn't want to say anything. But right then he thought God was one for two for the day. He carefully tried the bike and decided it was OK.

"See you at home, big guy," his father said.

His father passed him before Daniel was even out of the parking lot. When he got home, only his mother's and his brother's cars were there. Jim was in the driveway shooting baskets.

"Hey, hotshot," Jim said, firing the ball at him. "Shoot a few?"

"Nah."

"C'mon! You never want to play anymore. You gettin' too old for me or something?"

"Nah. I really don't feel like playing right now."

"Suit yourself, Dan."

"Where's Mom and Dad? I saw 'em leave the home."

"Here and gone," Jim said, shooting long. "On an errand. Home soon."

Daniel wandered inside. Something good was in the oven, but he couldn't guess what it was. Maryann sat on the sofa, drying her nails. "Date tonight?" Daniel asked.

"I wish. Nope. Just want 'em to look nice."

Daniel shrugged. "Let me know when Mom and Dad get here, will you?" he asked, heading for the stairs.

Maryann grunted.

Just before he went into his room, he yelled back down the stairs. "Hey, Mar, what's this junk in the hall by Dad's office?"

"He's just cleaning it out a little, Dan!" she said. "Moving some stuff to the basement! Just leave it there!"

Daniel flopped onto his bed and put his hands behind his head. He stared at the ceiling until he couldn't keep his eyes open. He was dozing when he heard car doors slam. He decided to wait until he was called to dinner before going back downstairs.

In a few minutes he heard a knock at his door. It was his mother. She came in and sat in a chair next to his bed. "You ready for some dinner, dear?" she asked softly.

"Yeah," he said, stretching and sitting up.

"Follow me," she said, "and don't say anything."

He was puzzled, but he was also still half asleep. He followed her down the hall, between the boxes, to his dad's office. She pushed open the door and he looked in. The room had been made over into a bedroom with lacy curtains and frilly bedcovers.

"Your sister is moving into here," Mom said.

"What's wrong with *her* room?" Daniel asked.

His mother put a finger to her lips. Then she led him downstairs. Sitting at the dinner table, right next to his place, was his little Mexican friend.

"Yolanda!" he said, still trying to make sense out of everything.

She stopped chatting with Maryann and Jim. Her eyes grew large. She stood, staring at Daniel. "This is the other brother?" she asked, gasping.

Everyone nodded and smiled.

"Daniel!" she cried, running to him. *"You got me after all!"*